Your Friend, Annie

Written and Illustrated by
Carole Katchen

AN
APPLE
PAPERBACK

SCHOLASTIC INC.
New York Toronto London Auckland Sydney

ISBN 0-590-42732-6

12 11 10 9 8 7 6 5 4 3 2   0 1 2 3/9

Printed in the U.S.A.   40

First Scholastic printing, December 1989

This book is for all the kids:
Alex, Becky, Cliff, both Heathers, Jodi,
Josh, Lee and Max, and of course, Colleen.
With a special thanks to Brigid Crosby,
Bahram, and Greg Holch.

Dear Colleen,

Here I am in Santa Marita, California. You are probably thinking, "What is she doing in Santa Marita? She said she was moving to Los Angeles."

Well, Santa Marita *is* Los Angeles, sort of. See, there are all these different little towns like Westwood and Beverly Hills and Hollywood and they are all lumped together in one big city and that is Los Angeles.

It's really weird. You drive and drive and drive and you never get out of town. There are no fields or farms, just streets and houses and stores forever until you run into the ocean.

Remember how I said I was going to hate it? Well, I do! I wish I was back in Cottonwood with you, but do my parents ever ask what I want? No!

Your friend,

Annie

Moving to California.

Dear Colleen,

Yesterday we had a picnic at the beach. My brothers kept jumping around, shouting, "Oh, boy, we're going to the beach!" Big deal. I mean, what's a beach anyway but a lot of sand?

The sand got in everything — in my hair, in my ears, in between my toes, in my book, even in the sandwiches and potato salad. Maybe that's why they're called sandwiches. My brothers can't wait to go back. Yuck, puke!

There were lots of kids there, but none of them talked to me, even when I said hello to them.

I wish we'd never moved.

Your friend,

Annie

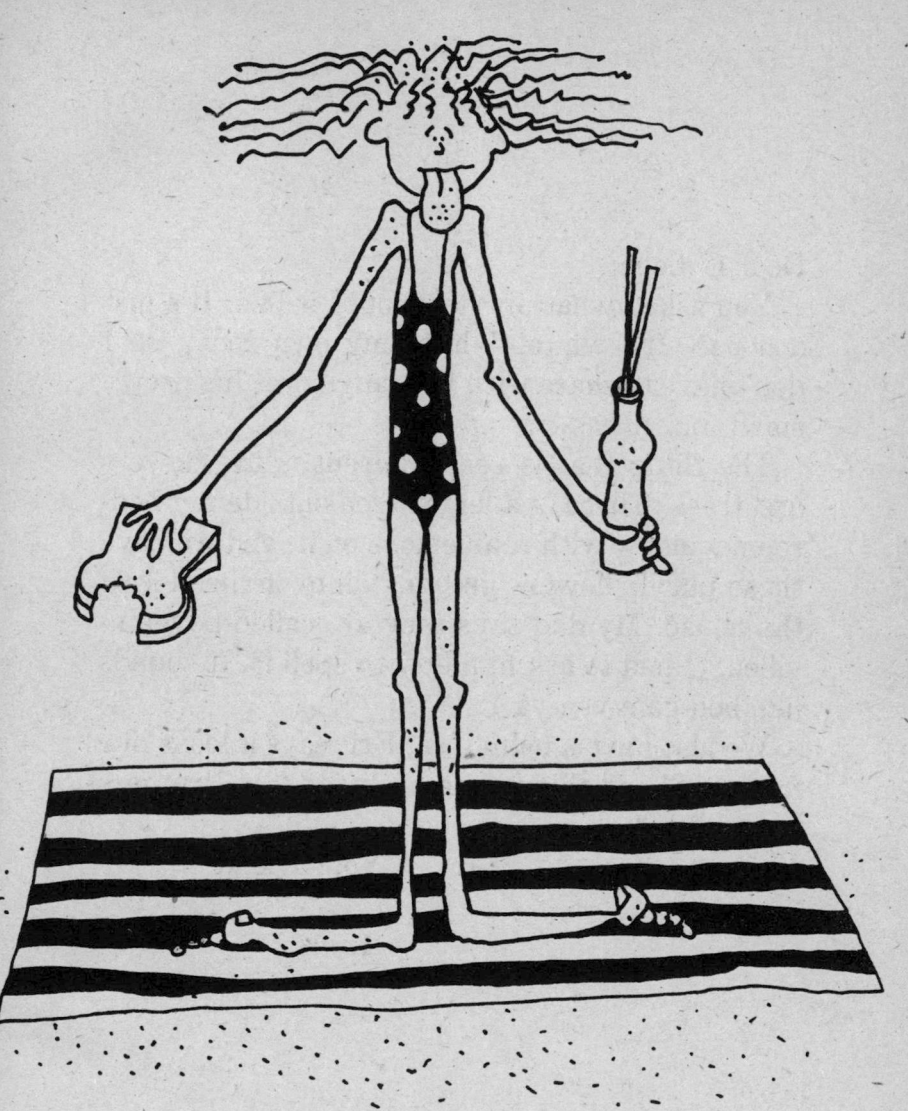

Here I am at the beach.
See all the sand? You can have it.

Dear Colleen,

You asked what my new house is like. It's just a house. It's white. I have my own room, so I don't have to share with Eric anymore. It's pretty small, but it has two windows.

The thing that is real different is the flowers and trees. There is a lemon tree outside my bedroom window with real lemons on it, and we have these purple flowers growing all over the side of the house. My dad says they are called bougainvillea. (I had to ask him how to spell it. It sounds like boo-gain-vee-ya.)

We also have a palm tree. Eric says it looks like me — tall and skinny and bushy on top. Brothers are so dumb.

Your friend,

Annie

Me and a palm tree. How depressing!

Dear Colleen,

Summer camp sounds like fun, and I'm glad you had a good time. I wish I could go to camp. Or something. There is nothing to do here.

I go to the library a lot. I just got a book about Guatemala. There is a place there called Chichicastenango, and they have a big market outside where they sell baskets and chickens and vegetables and shoes and everything.

Most of the people are Indians. They are short and have dark hair and they wear costumes made from lots of bright colors — red and blue and yellow and purple and green.

When I grow up and become an artist, I would like to go there and paint all those colors. I want to go everyplace interesting.

Do you think they would think I was weird there? With my red hair, I mean. Maybe I could wear an Indian costume, but probably it would be too short, and my knees would stick out. I wish I wasn't so tall.

Your friend,

Annie

Shopping in Chichicastenango.

Dear Colleen,

Saturday I went shopping on Rodeo Drive with my mother and grandmother. They pronounce it Row-*day*-oh. It's just a street with shops on it, but it's in Beverly Hills and all the movie stars go shopping there.

My mother and grandmother kept looking for movie stars. We had lunch in a restaurant, and they were so busy looking around for stars that they hardly ate anything. They looked like ostriches — you know how ostriches twist their heads all around on their necks? It was very embarrassing.

I ate a hamburger. It wasn't very good.

They didn't see any movie stars.

Your friend,

Annie

*Don't ever have lunch with my mother
and grandmother on Rodeo Drive!*

Dear Colleen,

Thanks for your letter. Here are the answers to your questions.

Yes, you can come to Guatemala with me. Start saving your allowance.

No, there aren't any kids on my block. I mean, there are kids, but they are all little like my brother Billy, and who wants to play with them?

Yes, it's very hot here. We have air-conditioning, but it broke down the other day, and my dad yelled a lot.

How is your dog?

Your friend,

Annie

These are the kids on our block.

Dear Colleen,

I'm sorry Skipper has mange. What is mange?

My mom took me shopping for some school clothes. We didn't go to Rodeo Drive. We went to a shopping mall, and we didn't see any movie stars there, either.

There were lots of kids there, but they were all too busy shopping to talk to me.

I got some new jeans. The saleslady said all the kids are getting them for school. They are very tight. I hope they don't make me look too skinny.

Did you get any new school clothes?

Your friend,

Annie

My new TIGHT jeans.

Dear Colleen,

Thanks for telling me what mange is. I don't think I would like to have my hair fall out in great big globs. Is Skipper embarrassed to go out with the other dogs?

No, I haven't decided what clothes I am taking to Guatemala. Your new school dress sounds great. Yes, you can bring it to Guatemala if you want, but it might get squashed in your suitcase.

No, I don't ride my bicycle much. There is no one to ride with and it's too hot and there's no place to go and my mother says the traffic is too dangerous. I wish I could ride my bike out to Hiller's farm with you and look at the new horses. They must be getting pretty big by now.

We are going to Disneyland next weekend. I hope it's fun.

Your friend,

Annie

*Poor Skipper! Are you
saving his hair that falls out?*

Dear Colleen,

Going to Disneyland was a disaster. We were driving there on the freeway, and we got in a terrible traffic jam. All the cars just stopped. You wouldn't believe it. There were all these cars just sitting there in the road. It was like the pumpkins in Mr. Marsh's field just before Halloween, only instead of pumpkins they were cars.

After a long time the cars finally started moving, but then they stopped. Then they started again and then they stopped again.

Eric kept saying he was hungry and Billy had to go to the bathroom. Then smoke started coming out of our car, and we had to turn off the air-conditioning. It was gross.

Then the cars started moving again, but ours wouldn't start and everybody started honking at us. My dad had to walk to a phone to call a tow truck to come and get us. We ate some candy bars in the gas station and watched them fix our car. Then we went home.

My dad says he loves being in California, but he sure yells a lot here.

Your friend,

Annie

On the way to Disneyland.

Dear Colleen,

We went to Disneyland again. This time we got there without our car breaking down. It was pretty much fun. My favorite ride was Pirates of the Caribbean. We had to wait in a lot of lines, and Billy threw up. Dad didn't yell this time, but Mom started crying. Parents are weird.

No, I guess dogs don't really get embarrassed even if their hair is falling out. Dogs are lucky. They don't have to worry about other dogs laughing at them. Do you suppose dogs ever get lonely? Maybe it would be nice to be a dog.

I think it is hot in Guatemala; so you probably don't need to bring your boots and mittens.

Your friend,

Annie

They made me wear
these dumb mouse ears!!

Dear Colleen,

My grandmother came over yesterday with a bag of avocados she picked off her tree. She lives in another little town that's part of Los Angeles, but you have to drive forever to get there.

She asked why I was sitting in the house reading instead of outside playing with some kids. I told her I like reading and besides, there aren't any kids for me to play with.

My mother says when school starts, I will make lots of new friends. I'm not so sure. I mean, how do you make friends anyway? In Cottonwood I never had to make friends; they were just always there.

Your friend,

Annie

Gramma in her jeans picking avocados.

Dear Colleen,

I am reading a book about Alaska. It says there are places there where in the winter it almost never gets light, and in the summer it almost never gets dark. That's because it's so far north. Isn't that weird? I mean, how would you be able to sleep if it never got dark?

In some places in Alaska it is so cold that the snow and ice never melt, and there are no roads or anything. People used to have dogsleds so they could go places; now they mostly use snowmobiles like we used to ride in Cottonwood in the winter.

My dad says it never snows in Los Angeles. He says that's great because he won't ever have to shovel snow off the driveway here. I don't think it's so great. How can you have winter if you don't have snow?

Your friend,

Annie

Nighttime in Alaska in the summer.

Dear Colleen,

Today we went shopping for school clothes again. We mostly bought socks and underwear and things. We went to a different shopping mall — there sure are a lot of them.

School starts in three weeks. My mother took me there to register, and I met the principal. Her name is Mrs. Lindberg, and she is pretty nice. I didn't meet my teacher yet. Her name is Miss Li. That's a Chinese name. I'm going to get a book at the library about China.

The school building is not like our school in Cottonwood with two floors. It's kind of flat and all spread out and it's very big. I hope I don't get lost.

No, I don't think I want to go to Alaska. I can't figure out how to draw snow.

Your friend,

Annie

See? My snow looks like sand.

Dear Colleen,

Sunday my dad took us to the Venice Boardwalk. What a wild place that is! There were millions of people walking along this kind of street by the beach, and on both sides there were other people selling clothes and sunglasses and playing music and cooking food and just being crazy.

There was an amazing juggler there. First he juggled plain things like balls and apples. Next he threw these big knives in the air. It was scary — I thought he was going to cut himself, but he didn't. Then he took out a chainsaw, like the one your father uses to cut down trees, and he turned on the motor and he threw it up in the air and juggled it with other things.

There were lots of weird-looking people there. One man wore a white robe and a white turban and he was roller-skating and playing a guitar. Lots of people were on skates. I think I'll get my roller skates out.

Your friend,

Annie

The Venice Boardwalk.

Dear Colleen,

I know I never learned to roller-skate in Cottonwood. You don't have to remind me. But maybe I'll do better in California. Anyway it's something to do.

My mother started taking a cooking class. She said it's a sushi class. I was so excited, I thought it must be something fabulous like brownies or pizza. No such luck! Do you know what sushi is? Raw fish! Yuck, puke! I'm not eating any. It might kill me.

Good luck on your first day of school. Are you wearing your new dress? Say hi to Kevin for me. Write and tell me all about Mr. Larkin.

Your friend,

Annie

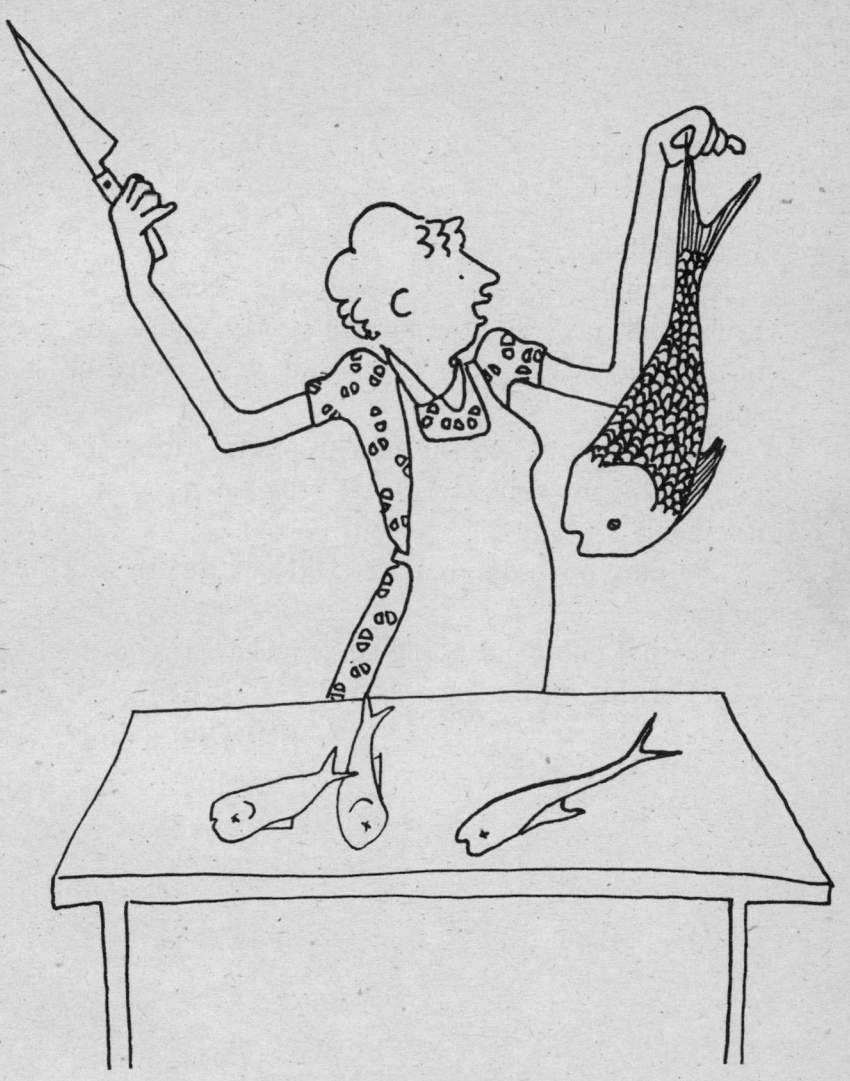

Does this look like a
normal mother to you?

Dear Colleen,

How could you just sit there and stare at Mr. Larkin all day? I know he has pretty blue eyes, but *all day?* Didn't he think you were weird or something?

I wish I could see the lunchroom now that it's painted bright yellow. I bet it's like sitting inside a lemon.

The new boy sounds cute. Did you get to talk to him?

I wish I could be going to school with you instead of this dumb, new school.

Your friend,

Annie

*Colleen's first day at school
— gaga over Mr. Larkin!*

Dear Colleen,

I am still roller-skating, sort of. I'm not very good yet, so my mother bought me some knee pads — she said she was tired of looking at my bloody knees.

I finally saw a movie star. In the grocery store, can you believe it? It was Lance Kane; you know, the doctor on the TV show *County Hospital*. We were in the vegetable section near the cabbages and my mother whispered to me, "Look over there! It's Lance Kane, the actor!"

So I looked, but all I saw was this bald guy, and I said, "Where? All I see is that bald guy."

And she said, "That's him! He wears a wig on TV. Lots of actors do."

How disappointing. Now when I watch TV, all I look at is the actors' hair to see if it's real or not.

Just ten days until school starts.

I ate some raw fish. I didn't die.

Your friend,

Annie

This is a movie star?

Dear Colleen,

Someone stole the stereo out of my father's car, so he got a new stereo, and he got a burglar alarm put in the car, too. Last Tuesday night when we were all asleep, there was suddenly this awful, loud noise — *Woo-ee-oo-ee-oo-ee!* Like a fire engine was driving through our living room.

It woke everybody up, and my dad went outside in his pajamas to see what was happening. He came back in and said it was a cat walking on the car that made the burglar alarm go off. He said, "Well, at least I know that nobody will steal my car stereo now."

The next day while he was at work, somebody stole his car stereo.

Your friend,

Annie

Dad hunting burglars.

Dear Colleen,

I'm glad you had fun at Susie's birthday party. I wish I'd been there. Yes, that is too bad that the prize you won was barrettes when you just got your hair cut short. Maybe you can let it grow long again.

Did Frankie really kiss Michelle? I bet she was mad.

I don't like white cake, either. For my birthday I always ask for chocolate.

I don't know why my school starts after yours. I guess it's just because it's California.

It's okay if you don't answer every single one of my letters. Probably after my school starts, I won't have so much time to write letters, either.

Your friend,

Annie

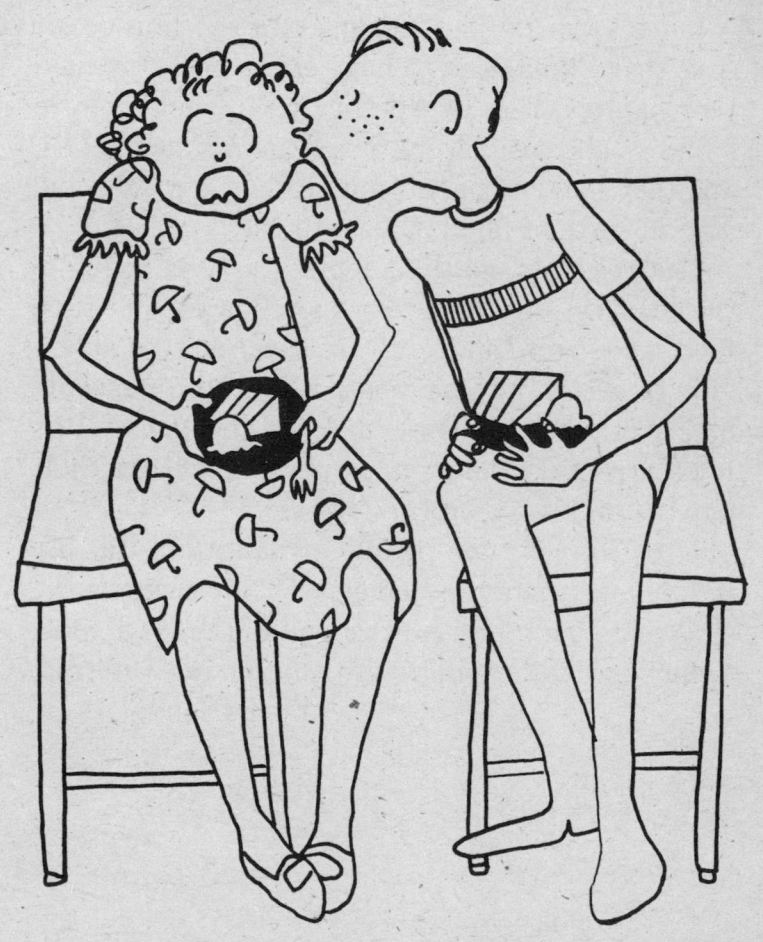

Frankie kissing Michelle.

Dear Colleen,

I got a book about China from the library. It says that China used to have emperors who ruled the country. They were very rich. They lived in palaces, and they wore jewels and fancy robes, and they had lots of servants to take care of them and all sorts of fancy things to eat.

The peasants, all the people who were living in the countryside, were very poor. They didn't have food, and their children were sick. But the rulers didn't care about the peasants, so the peasants had a revolution. They took all the money and jewels from the rulers and made them leave their palaces and work on the farms.

I see lots of poor people in Santa Marita. My father calls them the homeless. They sleep on the sidewalks, and they eat food out of the trash bins. I wonder if there will be a revolution in California.

Your friend,

Annie

*I'm glad I don't have to sleep on
the sidewalk like homeless people do.*

Dear Colleen,

Last night my dad took me into the living room after dinner so we could have what he calls a "heart-to-heart" talk. We sat down on the couch and he said, "I know it's been hard for you to leave all your friends and come to a brand-new place."

I nodded.

He went on, "Cottonwood is a nice place for kids. It's small and friendly, and there are woods and farms and animals."

I nodded.

Then he said, "But Cottonwood isn't the whole world. Your mother and I wanted you kids to know what a big city is like, too. Then when you grow up, you can choose what kind of place you want to be in and what kind of life you want to live."

I nodded.

He said, "I am sure you are scared about starting a new school, but you will be just fine."

I nodded.

Then he stood up and said, "I'm glad we had this talk. It is very important to communicate."

Your friend,

Annie

A heart-to-heart talk.

Dear Colleen,

Well, tomorrow is the big day. I start Rosedale Elementary School in the sixth grade. How gross!

Remember when we used to dream about being sixth-graders? We would be the bosses. We could help the teachers and tell all the little kids what to do. And we would have dreamy Mr. Larkin for our teacher. It was going to be so great.

Oh, well.

Your friend,

Annie

Getting ready for school tomorrow.

Dear Colleen,

Yesterday was the worst day of my life! I got all dressed up for the first day of school like we always did in Cottonwood, and I went to school and I was the only one in my class who was dressed up. Everybody else was wearing jeans, and some kids were even wearing shorts. Well, there were a few other girls in dresses, but they didn't speak English.

Then when it was lunchtime, I went to the coatroom to get my lunch. I took my sack down from the shelf, and I dropped my milk money on the floor. So I put my lunch on a chair for just a second and somebody sat on it. Can you believe it? Somebody sat on my lunch!

And then I went to the bathroom and I got lost and by the time I got back to my class, everybody was already sitting down, and the whole class laughed at me.

I hate school.

Your friend,

Annie

My lunch — as flat as a pancake!

Dear Colleen,

The rest of the week at school wasn't so bad. I wore jeans every day.

My teacher is pretty nice. I asked her if she comes from China because she has a Chinese name. She said, no, she was born in San Francisco. That's another city in California. I told her I was reading a book about China, and she said maybe I could make a report on it.

I asked if her grandparents were emperors or peasants in China. She said her family was very poor, so they came to America to help build the railroads.

I think she is very beautiful. I never knew a Chinese-American person before.

Your friend,

Annie

Miss Li. Isn't she pretty?

Dear Colleen,

I sit next to a girl named Rochelle. She is tall like me, but she isn't skinny, and she has beautiful blonde hair. She hangs around with two other girls named Toni and Marissa, and they seem to have a lot of fun. They are always laughing. I think I would like to have them for my friends.

I say "hi" to Rochelle every day when we sit down. Sometimes she says "hi" back. I don't know what else to say to her. I'll have to think of something.

Your friend,

Annie

Rochelle and Toni and Marissa.

Dear Colleen,

Yesterday when I got home from school, there was a jar on my dresser. I picked it up to see what was inside, and there was this gross spider looking at me. It started to move and I screamed and dropped the jar and it broke and the spider got loose.

Billy came into my room and said, "Did you see my spider? Isn't it awesome?"

He got mad because I let his spider loose. Finally he caught it again and put it in another jar.

Billy *loves* California because there are so many bugs here. *Blech!*

Your friend,

Annie

Billy and his pet spider. Yuck!

Dear Colleen,

We have busing at my school. Some of the kids live close to the school like me and walk there every day, but some kids come on buses from all over the city. Some kids are black and some kids are Asian. There are two boys from Iran, one girl from El Salvador, a girl from Vietnam, and one from France. I like that.

When I lived in Cottonwood, I thought everybody was pretty much the same. I didn't know there were so many different kinds of people right here in the United States.

Your friend,

Annie

The kids in my class are all different,
like a bunch of different flowers.

Dear Colleen,

Today on the way to lunch I said to Rochelle, "It sure is awful being tall, isn't it?"

She said, "No. I like it. Lots of movie stars are tall."

Then she went to sit with Toni and Marissa. There was no room for me at their table, so I sat next to Rami, a boy from Iran. We traded part of our lunch.

He brought his lunch in this weird lunch box thing. There were three metal dishes stacked on top of each other with a cover on top, and it was all held together by the handle. He said all the kids have them in Iran.

In the top dish there was yogurt and fruit. Under that was bread and some vegetables. And in the last dish was rice with some meat and sauce. He let me taste everything. I liked the rice stuff best.

I gave him half my peanut butter sandwich.

Your friend,

Annie

Sharing lunch with Rami.

Dear Colleen,

I started reading a book about Iran. Iran used to be called Persia, and that's where Persian rugs come from. The religion is Islam. People pray many times a day, and women have to wear a long black dress that even covers their hair. It's called a *chador*. I would like to go there and paint pictures of women in a *chador*.

I don't have as much time to read anymore, because we have lots of homework.

I still roller-skate sometimes. I am better, but I still fall down a lot. There is a house down the street with a great big driveway. I practice there. I don't know who lives there. I never see anyone.

Your friend,

Annie

*Here I am wearing a chador
and roller-skating in Iran.*

Dear Colleen,

Today I had a conversation with Rochelle. We were walking to gym and I said, "I am reading a book about Iran."

She said, "Why?"

I said, "Because it's interesting. I like to know about different places."

She said, "Oh."

Is this how you make friends?

Your friend,

Annie

A conversation with Rochelle.

Dear Colleen,

Yes, you can come to Iran with me.

No, I don't know if I will go to Guatemala first or to Iran first.

Yes, I know you like hot fudge sundaes, but if you spend all of your money on ice cream, you won't have any money to go to Guatemala *or* Iran.

Maybe you should make a budget. That's what my grandmother was saying to my mother because my mother was saying everything is too expensive in Los Angeles, and she is always running out of money.

My grandmother said first you write down how much money you have every week. Then you write down all the things you *absolutely need to buy* for the week, and how much they cost. You subtract from your allowance the things you need, and then what is left you can spend on anything you want.

Your friend,

Annie

*Colleen making a budget. Is this
what your new short hair looks like?*

Dear Colleen,

My mother is taking a new cooking class. This one is even weirder than the one with raw fish. In this class she is learning how to cook with flowers. Flowers! Like in the garden. Last night I looked down at my salad and in the middle of the lettuce was a red nasturtium.

I said, "What is this flower doing here?"

She said, "It's part of your salad. Eat it."

"Are you kidding?" I said. "I can't eat that. It might kill me."

She said, "It won't kill you. Eat it."

I ate part of it. It tasted like pepper. Tonight we are having fried zucchini blossoms. Why can't she just learn how to make brownies?

Your friend,

Annie

Who ever heard of eating flowers?
Next we'll be eating Billy's bugs.

Dear Colleen,

Well, if you *absolutely need* to eat hot fudge sundaes, I guess you will have to spend your allowance on that. Maybe you can get a part-time job to earn money for traveling.

My brother Eric got a skateboard. All of the boys here ride them, even the big boys older than me. Eric's friends built a ramp for their skateboards. It's like a hill made out of wood. They go rolling down the sidewalk as fast as they can. Then they ride up to the top of the ramp and go flying off in the air. Some of the bigger boys do a flip in the air. Then they land on their skateboards and keep rolling down the sidewalk.

My mom is worried that Eric will break his arm or something, but Dad says, "Sharon, you can't worry about every little thing. Eric will be fine."

Your friend,

Annie

The skateboarders.

Dear Colleen,

Today I ate lunch with Rochelle and Toni and Marissa. There was an empty seat at their table, so I sat there.

Mostly they talked about clothes. They were laughing at a girl named Marsha because her jeans didn't have the right label. They said the *only* kind of jeans that are any good are Guess jeans. That is what they all wear.

I was glad I was wearing a skirt today because my jeans are the wrong kind.

Your friend,

Annie

Looking at everybody's clothes.

Dear Colleen,

Gee, I don't know what kind of job you could get. How about baby-sitting or maybe feeding Mrs. Holloway's chickens?

Eric broke his arm skateboarding yesterday. He asked me to draw a picture on his cast. I drew him falling off the skateboard.

I got an *A* on my spelling test today. I am doing pretty well in all my subjects except computers. We have a computer lab in my school. All the other kids have been using computers for years, but I never even saw one before I came here. The other kids play games on them and everything. I feel very stupid.

Your friend,

Annie

Eric breaking his arm.

Dear Colleen,

After dinner last night I asked my mother if I could get some new jeans. She asked what was wrong with the ones I already have. I told her they have the wrong label, that all the kids wear Guess jeans.

"Guess jeans?" my mother said. "I don't even buy Guess jeans for myself. Those are the most expensive ones in the stores."

My dad said, "Can't you just sew some new labels on your old jeans?"

Finally my mother said we'll go shopping Saturday and *maybe* get me some Guess jeans.

Your friend,

Annie

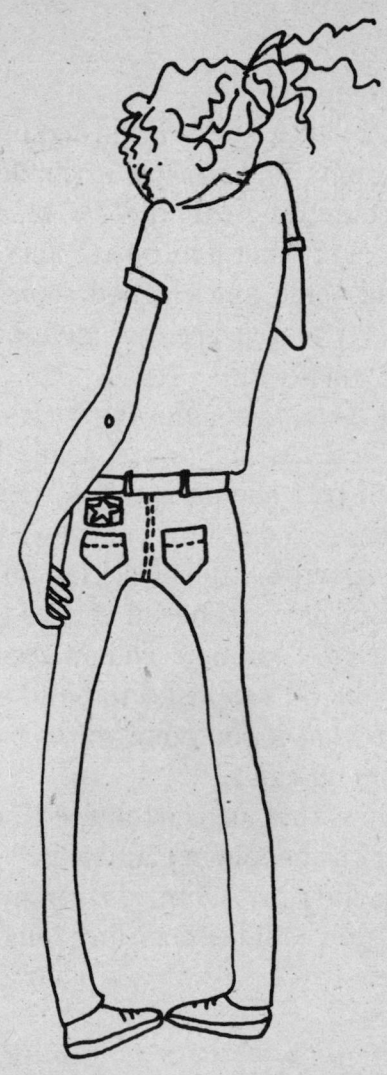

My jeans have the wrong label.

Dear Colleen,

I shared lunch with Rami again today; there was no room for me at Rochelle's table. He brought something called *chelo kebab*. It is made out of rice and meat and butter and egg yolks and onions and some spice called *somagh*. It looked weird, but it tasted great. I gave him part of my tuna fish sandwich.

I asked Rami if his mother wears a *chador*. He said, no, in L.A. she wears jeans like everyone else, but in Iran she used to wear a scarf over her hair and ears, and a long blouse with long sleeves and buttons up to the neck. It's the Islamic law that women have to be all covered up in public. He said the government leaders are very religious and everyone is supposed to be like them.

I asked what if someone wants to be different. He said you can't.

I told him that in Cottonwood people weren't as different as people in California. We didn't have any black kids or Asian kids or even kids from Iran. But you could choose any religion you want.

Your friend,

Annie

Rami telling me about Iran.

Dear Colleen,

I got some Guess jeans Saturday. Now maybe I can be friends with Rochelle and Toni and Marissa. It's very boring when you don't have friends, especially on weekends, when there is no one to play with.

I am still practicing roller-skating. I can almost turn in a circle without falling down.

That's too bad that Mrs. Holloway's chickens chased you away when you were trying to feed them. I'm sorry they ripped your new blue socks, but at least they didn't bite your leg.

Your friend,

Annie

Colleen and the vicious chickens.

Dear Colleen,

I wore my new jeans to school today, but Rochelle still didn't talk to me. I think I have the wrong kind of shoes. They all wear Reebok hightops. My shoes are Reeboks, but they're not hightops. In gym today they were laughing because Sandy has the wrong kind of shoes. They said she was a nerd, wearing bubble gum on her feet.

Eric is riding his skateboard again. Mom finally let him, even though he still has his cast on. His cast is gross. It's all gray and yukkie-looking. Billy likes it. He keeps asking if he can get a cast, too.

We are going to Universal Studios next weekend. They have a tour, and Dad is taking us. He says we'll get to see how they make movies and TV shows.

Your friend,

Annie

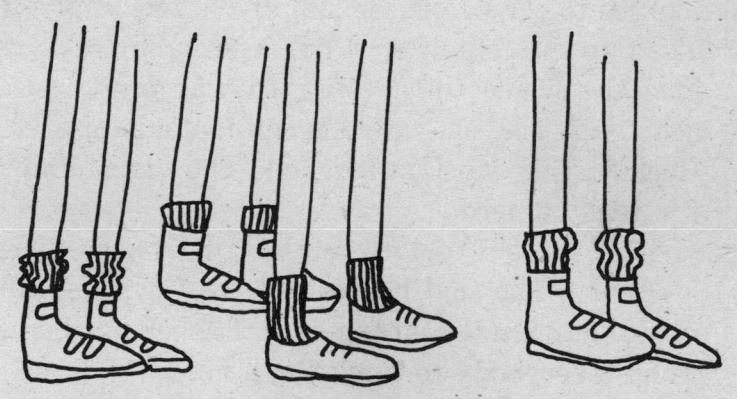

Everybody but me wearing high-tops.

Dear Colleen,

That's great that you started to play the oboe. What's an oboe?

I had a terrible time in school today. Miss Li took us to the computer lab, and when I put the disc into the computer, I put it in wrong and ruined the whole thing. Miss Li was pretty nice about it — she said anyone can make a mistake. Rochelle and Marissa laughed. They must think I'm really a nerd.

After school I told my mother that I need some high-tops. She said I already have Reeboks, but I said they are the wrong kind. I asked her if she wants everybody to think I'm a nerd.

Your friend,

Annie

*I think the computer is really an alien from
outer space, and it came to Earth to drive me crazy.*

Dear Colleen,

Universal Studios was very interesting. Did you know that when you see buildings in a movie, sometimes they aren't real buildings at all? At the movie studio they have whole streets that are just the fronts of houses and stores. They are called sets. There is nothing behind the fronts, but when you see them in the movies, they look like real houses.

They have all kinds of fake stuff. They can make it look like it's raining or snowing.

We saw Jaws, you know, the giant shark from the movie? I always thought it was a real fish in the ocean. It's really just a machine that looks like a fish, and it's not in the ocean; it's in a little lake.

And they had a show of a gunfight with stunt men, where all these guys got killed and fell off the buildings. Of course, I already knew people don't really get killed in movies.

Eric and Billy liked the stunt show best, and ever since we got home they have been shooting at each other and falling dead off the couch and chairs and things.

Your friend,

Annie

Eric and Billy practicing their stunts.

Dear Colleen,

I think it is very strange when you don't know if something is real or fake. When I watch movies now, I look at all the buildings and try to see around the corners to tell if it's a real building or just a set. Wouldn't it be weird if the whole world was that way with fake trees and fake buildings and fake rain?

Your friend,

Annie

What if all the trees were fake trees?

Dear Colleen,

Your oboe sounds neat. I never tried to play a musical instrument. Do you have to blow real hard to make music come out? What happens when you run out of breath?

Maybe you will learn how to play the oboe so well that people will pay you. Then you'll have enough money to go to Guatemala.

Your friend,

Annie

Colleen playing the oboe.

Dear Colleen,

Yesterday I told Rochelle I went to Universal Studios and asked if she ever was there. She said, "I went there twice. I am going to be a movie star."

I asked her how you get to be a movie star.

She said, "You have to be beautiful and meet the right people."

I asked, "Who are the right people?"

She said, "Producers and agents and other movie stars."

I told her I saw the actor Lance Kane.

She asked if I talked to him.

I said, "No."

She said, "Too bad."

Maybe if I met a movie star, I could be friends with Rochelle and Toni and Marissa. What do you think?

Your friend,

Annie

Rochelle plans to be a movie star.

Dear Colleen,

I guess it is hard to make your tongue work right when you play the oboe. I never thought much about tongues before. After I got your letter, I went in front of the mirror and tried making different shapes with my tongue. Then Eric walked into the bathroom and said I looked like an anteater.

I'm glad you have someone to practice your music with. I always thought Barbara was nice, even though we weren't friends. I didn't know she plays the flute.

Your friend,

Annie

*Does this look like
the tongue of an oboe player?*

Dear Colleen,

Next Sunday my parents are having a party. My father is inviting some people from work, and my mother is inviting some friends from her cooking class. They said Eric and Billy and I could bring some friends, too. I invited Rochelle and Toni and Marissa, but they said they have a previous engagement. They are all going to Marissa's beach house in Malibu. I wish I could go there.

I got a new book from the library. It is all about South America. It says the Amazon River goes all across the continent from Peru to Brazil. In some places it is so wide, you can't see the other side. The river has all kinds of fish in it, even piranhas. (That is pronounced pir-on-yas.) Piranhas have very sharp teeth and sometimes they eat people.

Your friend,

Annie

Paddling a canoe down the Amazon River.

Dear Colleen,

Yesterday after school I took a bus to Rodeo Drive. I walked around for three hours in my new high-tops. I got blisters on my feet, but I didn't see any movie stars.

Today I had lunch with Rami. He brought something called *tah chin*. It is rice and chicken and yogurt and eggs. It is yellow from a spice called saffron, and it tastes great. We shared. I gave him half of my bologna sandwich.

I told Rami I read a book about Iran and I would like to go there. He said I would like it because it is very interesting.

I think we should go to Guatemala first. It's closer. Iran is *very* far away.

Your friend,

Annie

Three hours and no movie stars.

Dear Colleen,

Miss Li assigned partners to everybody for a social studies project. My partner is Debbie Washington. She is an African American girl who rides the bus to school. She has black hair that is even curlier than mine and she has big, brown eyes.

We are supposed to give a report on a foreign country. Debbie said she would like to do a country in Africa.

Since we live so far apart, we are going to meet at a library in the middle on Saturday. I never knew a black person before. She seems nice.

Your friend,

Annie

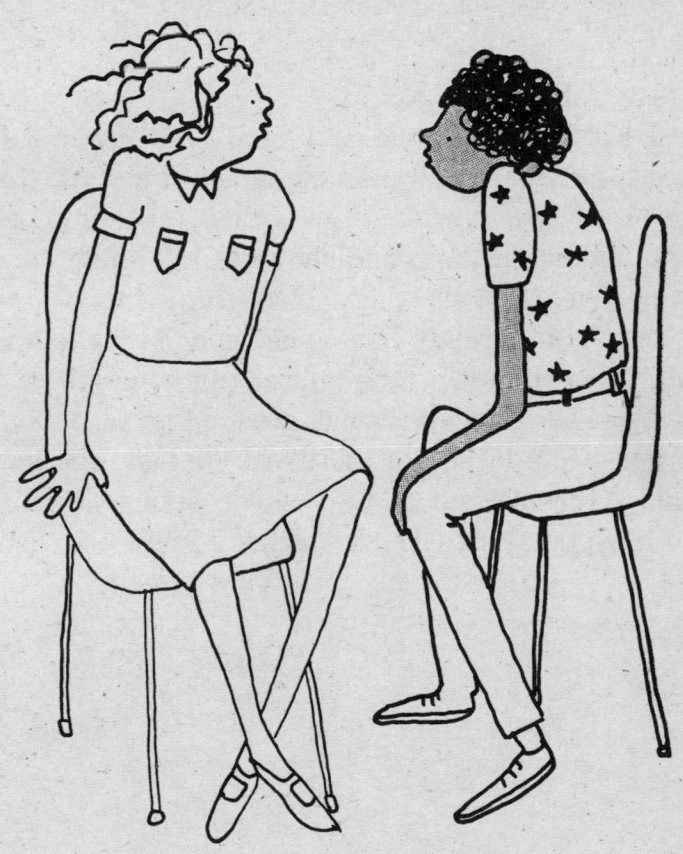

Me and my new work partner.

Dear Colleen,

I sat with Rochelle and Toni and Marissa at lunch today. They were talking about braces. Remember how Marianne got braces on her teeth and she hated them and she wouldn't smile for a whole year? Well, these girls think braces are great. Toni already has some, and Rochelle and Marissa are getting them later this year.

I asked Rochelle what was so great about braces. She looked at me like I was an idiot and said, "If you want to be a movie star, you have to have perfect teeth. Everybody knows that."

Your friend,

Annie

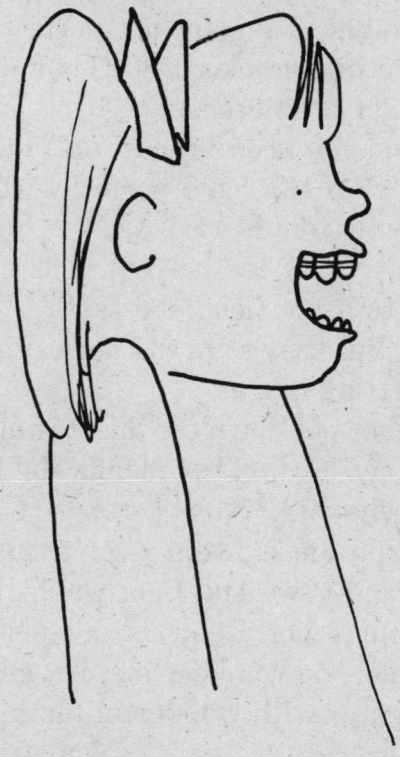

Toni showing off her braces.

Dear Colleen,

I looked at my teeth in the mirror for a long time last night. They are not perfect. One of my bottom teeth is crooked. So this morning I told my mother I need braces.

"What do you need braces for?" she asked.

I said, "So I can have perfect teeth. See, this one on the bottom is crooked."

She said, "Your teeth are just fine. You should be happy to have such good teeth."

I said, "But they're not. I need braces. Everybody is getting braces."

My mother put down the dish towel and put her hands on her hips. (That means she is very serious.) And she said, "Now, listen here, young lady. I bought you Guess jeans, even though your others are brand-new. And I got you high-tops, even though your other Reeboks are perfectly good. But I am not, do you hear me, not getting braces for a daughter with wonderful teeth."

Your friend,

Annie

"No braces!"

Dear Colleen,

I am glad you and Barbara are working on a report about the Civil War together. I am sure Mr. Larkin will like it and give you a good grade. But I don't know why she has to sleep over just so you can do a report.

My grandmother and I went looking at movie stars' houses. We bought a Star Map — that's a map that shows you where the movie stars live. We drove around all afternoon and saw lots of houses, but we didn't see any movie stars. How am I ever going to meet the right people?

You asked what Rami looks like. He is shorter than me, but he is kind of cute. He has brown eyes and a terrific smile; I don't know if he ever had braces. His hair is black and his skin is a little dark, like he always has a suntan. I bet he never gets freckles like me.

Your friend,

Annie

Me and Gramma, looking at a Star Map.

Dear Colleen,

My mother did the weirdest thing. She went with one of her friends from her cooking class to see a psychic. This is some lady who tells fortunes. It's a little weird that my mother wanted to have her fortune told, but what is really weird is that this woman tells fortunes from tongue prints.

She made my mother stick her tongue on some paper and then she looked at the paper and told my mother about the future. She said she could see my mother was going to take a long trip and fall in love with a dark-haired man.

My mother said, "Are you sure he doesn't have red hair? Harold, my husband, has red hair."

The woman said, "I only know what I see."

So my mother has been crying all day and saying she doesn't want to fall in love with a dark-haired man.

I hope my parents don't get divorced. That would be worse than moving to a new school.

Your friend,

Annie

Who ever heard of tongue prints anyway?

Dear Colleen,

Today in computer lab I was having a terrible time. I couldn't get the computer to work. I know there are three buttons you push, but I thought I was pushing the wrong buttons or pushing them in the wrong order or something. I was almost ready to cry when Rami came over and asked if he could help me.

I told him I can't ever remember how to make this computer work, and he turned it on for me. Somebody had pulled out the plug. No wonder it didn't work!

He said he will stay after school with me and help me learn how to work the computer. He says he knows about them because he got one when he was a little kid in Iran.

Your friend,

Annie

Rami coming to the rescue.

Dear Colleen,

Yesterday Rami met me in the computer lab after school. He showed me all the basic procedures, and then he made me keep going over them until I knew them myself. He didn't get tired or bored or anything. Then he showed me how to play a new computer game, and we played until they closed up the lab.

Eric gets his cast off next week. He is really excited. He says it makes his arm itch all the time like there are bugs crawling on him. I told him there probably *are* bugs crawling on him.

Your friend,

Annie

Eric itching.

Dear Colleen,

I stayed over at Debbie's house last night so we could work on our report. My dad took me over there. I felt a little weird riding to her house because all the people I saw in her neighborhood have dark skin. I wondered if they were all staring at me because I look different.

Debbie lives in a nice house. It has a big yard with lots of fruit trees. She has two brothers and her own room, just like me. She likes to read, too, and she has lots of books in her room.

While we were working on our report, we saw some pictures of African girls with their hair all in braids. We showed the pictures to Debbie's mother and she said she could braid our hair like that. It took a long time for her to do both of us because she had to make so many little braids.

I wore my hair to school that way today. Rochelle said I looked weird. I'm afraid she is never going to be my friend.

Your friend,

Annie

Debbie and me with African hairstyles.

Dear Colleen,

The greatest thing happened today! I was roller-skating at that house with the big driveway. I was practicing a figure eight on one foot. Just as I was starting the second loop, a car came down the driveway, and I lost my balance and crashed into the trash cans. I was so embarrassed, I thought I would die.

A man in the car asked me if I was okay. I didn't even look at him; I was so embarrassed.

I said, "I hope I didn't ruin your trash cans. I was trying to do a figure eight on one foot, but I don't think I am ever going to learn how to skate."

He said, "You're just leaning over too far. That's what my sister did before I taught her how to skate. I could show you how to keep your balance. Why don't you come over Thursday at four-thirty?"

I said, "Wow, that would be great." Then I looked up at him and you won't believe this! Do you know who it was? Johnny Victory! Johnny Victory, the singer! I have every one of his records.

I couldn't think of anything to say, and I know my face got all red the way it does, but he just waved and said, "See you Thursday."

Your friend,

Annie

Right into the trash cans.

Dear Colleen,

   This morning when I got to class, I told Rochelle that I met someone roller-skating.

   She said, "Roller-skating? How boring. Nobody roller-skates anymore." Then she said, "Who did you meet?"

   I said, "Johnny Victory."

   She jumped out of her chair and said, "Johnny Victory? *The* Johnny Victory? He's the best. You really met Johnny Victory?"

   At lunch she and Toni and Marissa made a place for me at their table. They spent all of lunch asking me about Johnny Victory. What does he look like? What does he sound like? How does he dress? What kind of car does he drive?

   When I told them I was going to see him again Thursday, they didn't say anything. They just sat there with their mouths open.

Your friend,

Annie

Rochelle was so excited!

Dear Colleen,

I went over to Johnny Victory's house at four-thirty. I was afraid he might forget, but he was there and had his skates on.

At first I just watched him skate. He can do spins and jumps and everything.

Then he started showing me how I can skate better. He said to keep my body up so I'll have good balance. Then he said I have to develop rhythm. He said it's just like dancing and he took my hands and skated backwards, pulling me, and he started singing. I almost died, it was so fabulous.

We skated for two hours and do you know, I can really skate better now.

When I told him thanks, he said it was fun. He asked if I would like to come to a recording session — would I ever! He wrote down my phone number and he said he'd call me.

Your friend,

Annie

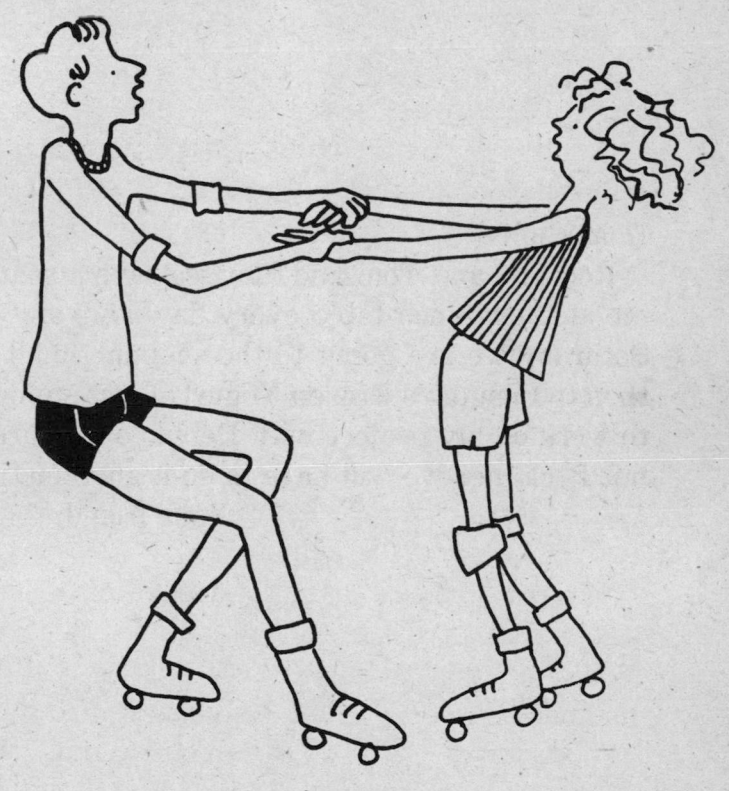

Can you believe it?
Just like in the movies.

Dear Colleen,

Rochelle and Toni and Marissa save a seat for me at their lunch table every day now, and this Saturday we are going to the shopping mall and then to Penguin's Frozen Yogurt. I was supposed to work on my project with Debbie on Saturday, but I told her we will have to do it another time.

Your friend,

Annie

They wanted to hear all the details.

Dear Colleen,

Rochelle invited me to her house after school Monday. We polished our fingernails.

Wednesday I invited her and Toni and Marissa to come to my house.

Toni asked, "Should we bring our suits to swim in your pool?"

I said, "We don't have a pool."

Marissa asked, "How about our tennis rackets? You have a tennis court, don't you?"

I said, "No."

Toni asked, "Well, what are we going to do there?"

I said, "We could play Monopoly or cards or listen to records."

Toni said, "Monopoly? I think I'll go home and wash my hair."

They didn't come over.

Your friend,

Annie

Polishing our nails.

Dear Colleen,

Eric got his cast off his arm, and he was so excited he tried a flip on his skateboard. He fell off and broke his arm again.

I bought a blue butterfly clip so I can pull my hair back like Rochelle. She says it looks chic. (That's pronounced sheek.)

Your friend,

Annie

Does this look chic?

Dear Colleen,

Rami asked me to sit with him at lunch today. He said he'd brought *chelo kebab* and he had enough for me. I said, "Thanks, but I have to sit with my friends."

He looked disappointed, and he said, "I thought I was your friend."

I told Rochelle and Toni and Marissa I was sorry that Rami felt bad. Rochelle said, "Who cares about him? He isn't even an American."

I hope Johnny Victory calls me to go to his recording session. Rochelle and Toni and Marissa want to meet him.

Your friend,

Annie

Rami at lunch.

Dear Colleen,

Marissa invited me to go to her beach house in Malibu this weekend with her and Rochelle and Toni. I don't know what you do at a beach house, but I'm sure it's fun.

Debbie is going to Chinatown this Sunday with her family. They are going to eat at a restaurant that serves *dim sum*. Debbie said *dim sum* is lots of little Chinese foods. Waitresses walk around with trays of different things to eat and you point to the ones you want. She said her mother would like me to come with them. I said I would like to, but I have a previous engagement.

Sure, I'll get you Johnny Victory's autograph if I see him again. And one for Barbara, too.

Your friend,

Annie

Debbie and me.

Dear Colleen,

I went to the beach house in Malibu. All we did for two whole days was try on clothes and fix our hair and sit in the sun — in the sand, which I hate. I kept wondering what *dim sum* tastes like. At Marissa's house we only ate salads because they say that's what movie stars eat.

Your friend,

Annie

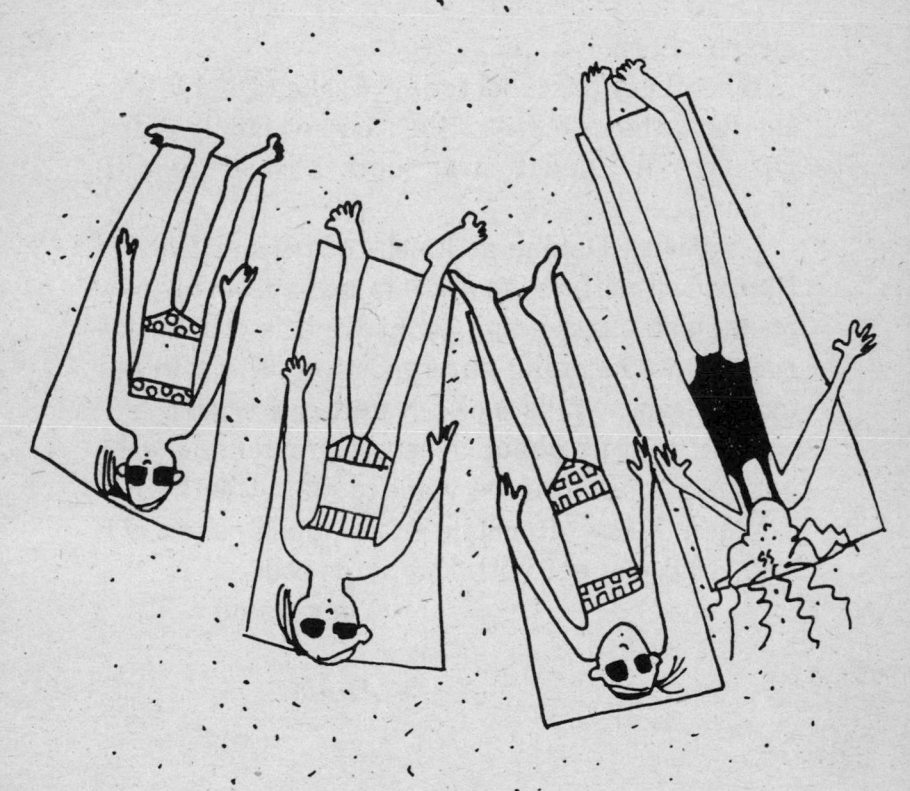

A day at the beach.

Dear Colleen,

When I got to school today, I asked Debbie how she liked the *dim sum*. She said her family didn't go. They decided to wait until I could go with them.

I sat with Debbie at lunch today, and I asked Rami to sit with us, too. We talked about this new book Debbie is reading about Nigeria. That's the country we're doing our report on. She said her mother can help us make Nigerian dresses.

Rami told us about a new computer game he got and he asked if we want to play it with him.

When I saw Rochelle after lunch, she said, "Why did you eat with the nerds today?"

Your friend,

Annie

Lunch with Debbie and Rami.

Dear Colleen,

Yesterday Johnny Victory called my house, and he invited me to come to the recording studio a week from Friday. He said I could bring some of my friends.

I am so excited. I don't know what to wear to a recording session. Probably my Guess jeans and high-tops and a sweatshirt.

I can't wait!

Your friend,

Annie

The fabulous phone call.

Dear Colleen,

Rochelle and Toni and Marissa are really excited about my phone call from Johnny Victory. They invited me to go get frozen yogurt with them after school today. I invited Debbie to come, too. The other three were ready to go, and I said, "We have to wait for Debbie."

Rochelle said, "Who invited her?"

I said, "I did."

Toni said, "She can't go with us."

"Why?" I asked.

"Why?" Toni said. "Just look at her. She's different."

Marissa said, "Well, I'm not going. I'm going home to wash my hair."

Debbie and I went alone.

Your friend,

Annie

Waiting for Debbie.

Dear Colleen,

At lunch today Rochelle told me that she and Toni and Marissa decided they don't want me to hang around with the nerds anymore.

"If you're going to be our friend," she said, "you have to be like us. You can't play with weird people."

I said, "You mean Debbie and Rami? You think they're weird?"

She answered, "They are very weird. If you want to be friends with us, you can't be friends with them."

Your friend,

Annie

Rochelle said I have to choose my friends.

Dear Colleen,

The recording session was fabulous! Johnny Victory introduced me to all the musicians. Then he kissed me, can you believe it! On my left cheek.

Afterwards my parents took us out for pizza, me and my friends — Eric and Billy and Debbie and Rami.

Remember when I was talking about real things and fake things? Well, I decided that Debbie and Rami are *real* friends. Rochelle and Toni and Marissa are *fake* friends. They look okay from the front, but if you peek around the corners, there is nothing there.

Your friend,

Annie

The recording session.

Dear Colleen,

I'm glad you like the photos Johnny Victory signed for you and Barbara.

I'm sorry you decided not to go to Guatemala, but maybe you're right — now that you and Barbara are musicians, it is important to stay home and practice.

Debbie said she would love to go to Guatemala, and maybe we can go to Iran and Nigeria, too. Rami wants to come, too.

I'll send you a postcard.

Your friend,

Annie

P.S. If you change your mind, you can come with us. Barbara, too.

*Me and my friends going off
to see the world.*

About the Author

Carole Katchen is a lot like Annie. She is tall and has frizzy hair. She recently moved to Los Angeles, where she hates the sand but likes to look for movie stars. She loves to travel to different countries and draw pictures of the people she sees there. She has written six other books; her favorite of those is *I Was a Lonely Teenager*.